The Birthday Party

by Frances Ann Ladd

Illustrated by Duendes del Sur

SCHOLASTIC INC.

New York Toronto London Auckland Sydney
Mexico City New Delhi Hong Kong Buenos Aires

It was Scooby-Doo's
birthday.
Shaggy was throwing him
a big party.
He got everything ready.
First he put up signs
and streamers.

Then he brought in food
from the grocery store:
pretzels, french fries,
drinks, and a tray
of fresh fruit.
"Pretty great!"
said Shaggy.

Shaggy put all the treats
on the table.
Then he wrapped
a present for Scooby.
He addressed the card:
To: Man's Best Friend
From: Dog's Best Friend

Shaggy set out
the ice-cream cake.
He even had prizes
to give the guests.
Everything was ready.

Scooby came
to the party.
But where was
the crowd?

"Jeepers!"
Shaggy cried.
"Where is my brain?
I forgot to invite
the guests!
Oh, brother!"

Scooby grinned.
He grabbed a treat.
Shaggy grinned, too.
"No problem!
More treats for us!"
said Shaggy.